D0604761

As I Was Crossing Boston Common

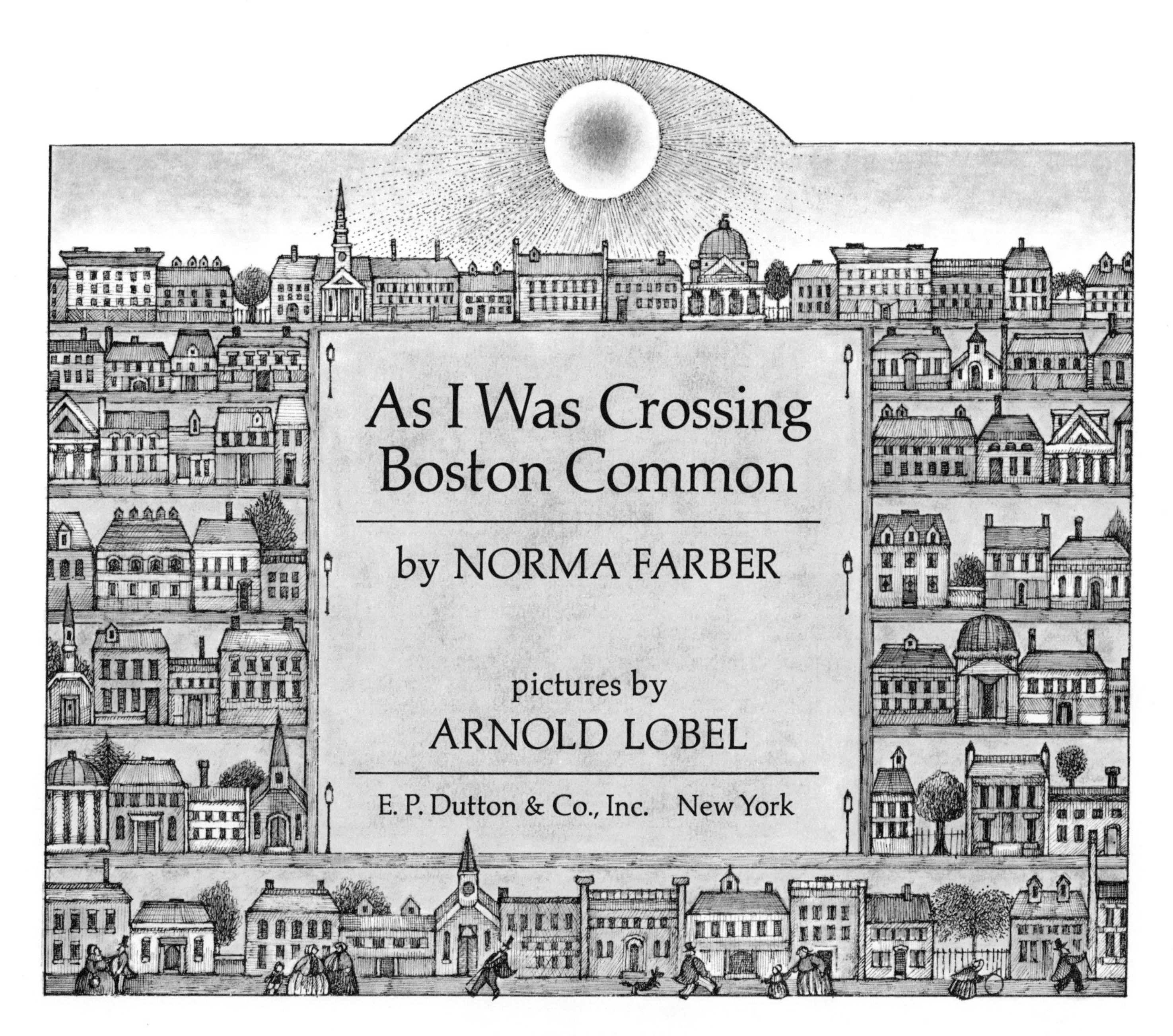

As I Was Crossing Boston Common

by NORMA FARBER

pictures by
ARNOLD LOBEL

E. P. Dutton & Co., Inc. New York

Library of Congress Cataloging in Publication Data

Farber, Norma As I was crossing Boston Common

SUMMARY: A rhymed account of all the unusual animals seen crossing Boston Common.

[1. Stories in rhyme. 2. Animals—Fiction]
I. Lobel, Arnold II. Title
PZ8.3.F224As [E] 75-6520 ISBN: 0-525-25960-0

Published simultaneously in Canada by Clarke, Irwin & Company Limited, Toronto and Vancouver

Designed by Riki Levinson
Printed in the U.S.A. First Edition
10 9 8 7 6 5 4 3 2 1

For Tom, who thought it most uncommon

As I was crossing Boston Common—

not very fast, not very slow—

I met a man with a creature in tow.
Its collar was labeled *Angwantibo.*
I thought it rather uncommon.

As I was crossing Boston Common—
not very fast, not very slow—
Angwantibo passed with a *Boobook* in tow,

Boobook passed with a *Coypu* in tow.
Where in the town were they going to go,
so seldom and uncommon?

As I was crossing Boston Common—
not very fast, not very slow—
Coypu passed with a *Desman* in tow,
Desman had an *Entellus* in tow,

Entellus, in turn, had a *Fennec* in tow,
where Boston folk went to and fro,
scanning the creatures from tip to toe,
and murmuring, "How uncommon!"

As I was crossing Boston Common—
not very fast, not very slow—
Fennec passed me, pulling a *Galliwasp*,
Galliwasp passed, with a *Hoopoe* in tow,

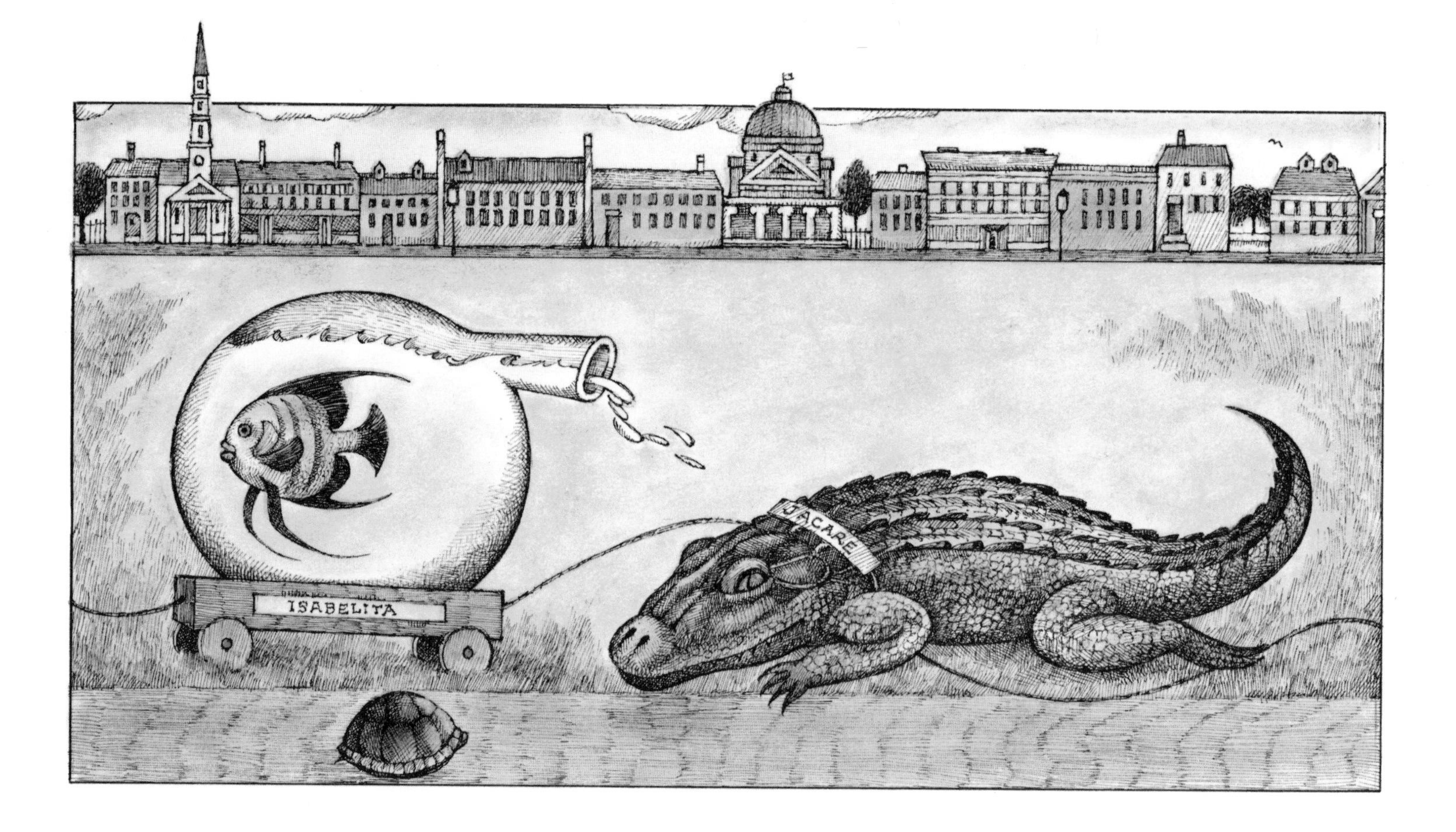

Hoopoe, an *Isabelita* in tow
(in a bowl with a spout—for the overflow).
The fish bowl pulled in tow a *Jacare*—

I snapped a picture, to prove it was so.
And everyone said, "How uncommon!"
"Uncommon!" cried pigeon, squirrel, crow,
and sparrows lined up in a common row.
"Most uncommon!"

As I was crossing Boston Common—
not very fast, not very slow—
Jacare passed me, pulling a *Kiang,*
Kiang was pulling a *Lory* in tow,

Lory was pulling in tow a *Mandrill,*
Mandrill was pulling a *Narwhale* in tow,
in a wagon heaped with ice and snow
(the rope being tied to his horn, in a bow).

Narwhale, riding, pulled an *Okapi*.
Where were they going? I wanted to know.
I looked for a reason, high and low,
for activity so uncommon.

As I slowed down on Boston Common—
not very slow, yet rather slow—
Okapi passed me, pulling a *Pudu*,

Pudu, passing, pulled a *Quirquincho,*
Quirquincho passed me, pulling a *Rhea,*

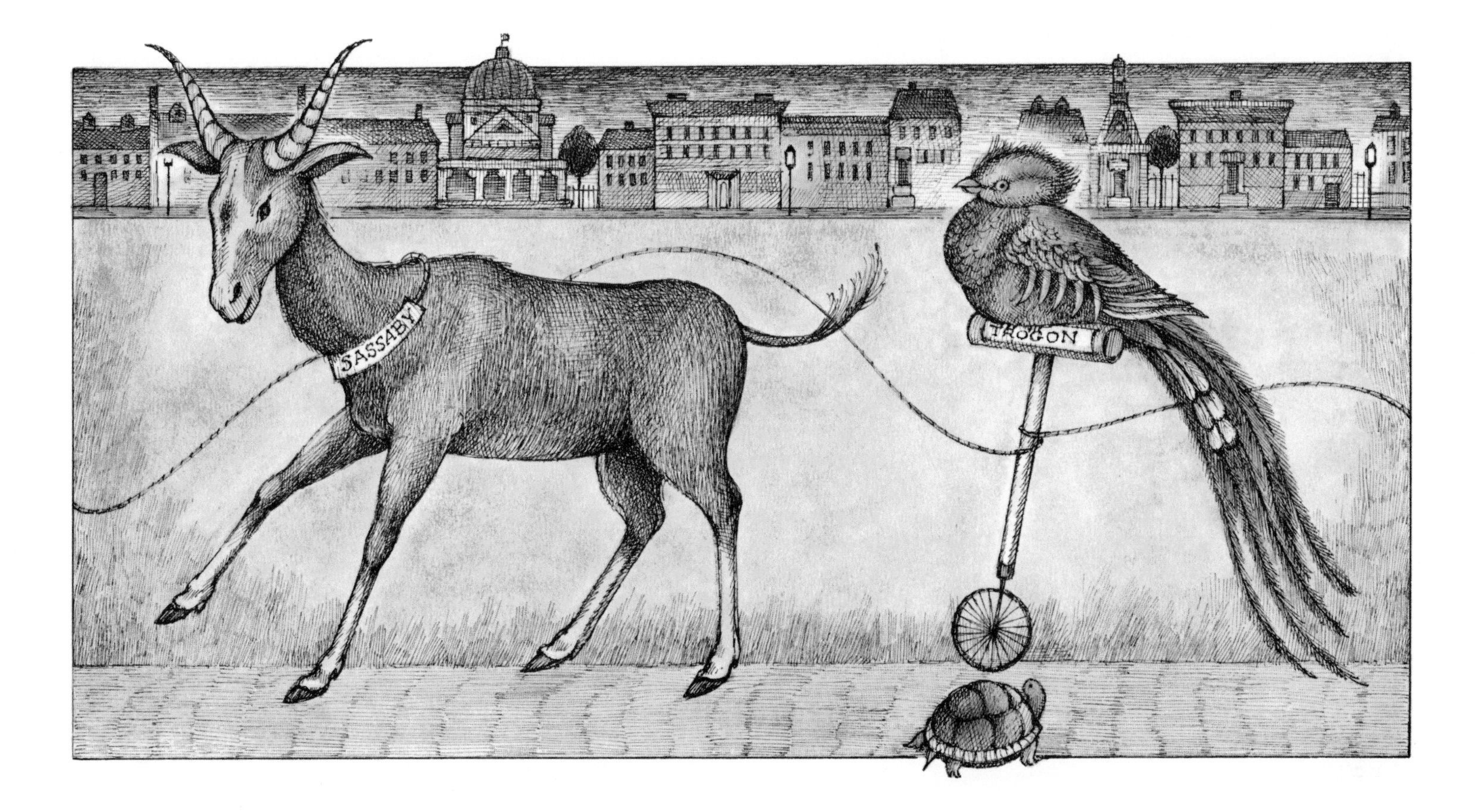

Rhea passed me, pulling a *Sassaby*,
Sassaby passed me, pulling a *Trogon*,

Trogon had an *Umbrette* in tow.
The line was long, and continued to grow.
A boy cried out, "Bravissimo!"
at the company so uncommon.

As I was dawdling on Boston Common—
slower than ever, slower than slow—
Umbrette came by with a *Vervet* in tow,
Vervet, in turn, was towing a *Wapiti*,

Wapiti pulled in tow a *Xenopus,*
Xenopus pulled on a *Yaguarundi,*
Yaguarundi was leading a *Zibet.*

Zibet — imagine! was leading a *man!* —
— the man who'd passed me a while ago!
He himself now looked uncommon.

YAGUAR
BOOBOOK
RHEA
JACARE

As I stood still on Boston Common,
they formed a circle, sweet and slow,
with everyone pulling someone in tow—
beginning with A for Angwantibo
in tow to the man, himself in tow—
sweet and slow, sweet and slow,
surprising and uncommon.

And round they went, and round, although
the dusk of Boston began to glow.
The lamps gave light enough to show
the turn of events was uncommon:
sweet and slow, a circular tow,
round as the moon that leaned to blow
its beams upon Boston Common.

Angwantibo (an-gwán-ti-boh) a small West African lemur

Boobook (boó-book) a small Australian owl

Coypu (kóy-poo) a South American rodent with webbed hind feet

Desman (dés-man) a Russian mole-like, water-loving animal

Entellus (en-téll-us) a long-tailed East Indian monkey

Fennec (fén-nec) a small African fox with large ears

Galliwasp (gáll-i-wasp) a harmless lizard of Jamaica

Hoopoe (hoó-poo) an Old World bird with a handsome crest

Isabelita (iz-a-bel-eé-ta) a highly colored West Indian angelfish

Jacare (já-ca-ray) a tropical American alligator

Kiang (kyáng) a Tibetan wild ass

Lory (ló-ri) an Australian parrot that feeds on honey and soft fruit

Mandrill (mán-drill) a large African baboon

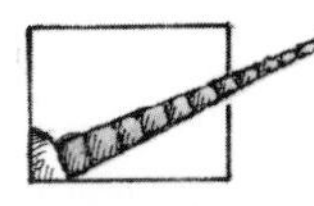

Narwhale (nár-whale) an Arctic sea mammal with a long, twisted, pointed tusk

Okapi (oh-ká-pi) a short-necked relative of the giraffe, from Africa

Pudu (poó-doo) a small, reddish deer with simple spike-like antlers

Quirquincho (kir-keén-choh) a small, hairy armadillo of South America

Rhea (reé-a) a South American ostrich with three toes on each foot

Sassaby (sáss-a-bi) a large, dark South African antelope with curved horns

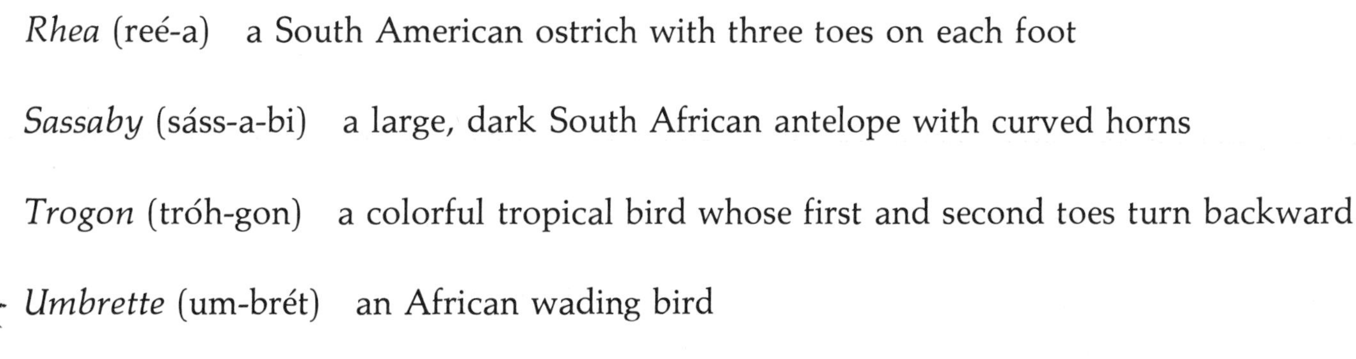

Trogon (tróh-gon) a colorful tropical bird whose first and second toes turn backward

Umbrette (um-brét) an African wading bird

Vervet (vúr-vet) a long-tailed African monkey

Wapiti (wó-pi-ti) the noble American elk, high as a horse

Xenopus (xén-oh-pus) a tongueless African toad

Yaguarundi (yag-war-ún-di) a grayish unspotted wildcat

Zibet (zí-bet) an East Indian civet cat

NORMA FARBER has "lived in and around Boston most of my life. And I've crossed Boston Common hundreds of times. Admittedly, *this* crossing was most uncommon...." She is a poet of distinction and a concert singer as well as the author of *Where's Gomer?*, a story about Noah's Ark, and *This Is the Ambulance Leaving the Zoo*, which has an alphabet theme. She says that "alphabet stories are special obsessions of mine—fascinated as I am with the beauty and expressiveness of the English language. The endlessly varied sounds of these animal names delight my musician's ear."

ARNOLD LOBEL has written and/or illustrated more than thirty books for children and is especially noted for his prize-winning books about Frog and Toad. He says about this book: "There was, in the mid-1800's, a special interest in nature in general and in strange species of animals in particular. I've always loved looking at these old bestiaries and it was my overall intention to work, on this book, for a sort of antiquarian ambience. As I don't know Boston too well, I did not attempt to depict a real place; this Common is a sort of anyplace of my imagination."

The display type was set in Palatino Foundry and the text type in Patina. The drawings are in ink with smudged pencil overlays for the color. The book was printed by offset at Halliday Lithographers.